W. M. Kirkland lives in Wiltshire, having worked/escaped across much of the UK and Europe. Now married with two children, Yogi a 7st Bulldog and Zeeki a small human, he spends most of his time trying to figure out what his IP Lawyer wife, Gem, does for a living. A keen fan of British ice hockey and all boxing, he has spent most of his life telling people he is an author. This book finally proves him right and means the score with Gem is around 13,877–1.

Gem – without you this would not have been possible. Without you, nothing much would have been possible. Well, nothing of note or value. Thank you for giving me the time, space and understanding to complete this.

I am one voice in a chorus of many.

W. M. Kirkland

Comedic Depression

Austin Macauley Publishers™
London • Cambridge • New York • Sharjah

A CIP catalogue record for this title is available from the British Library.

ISBN 9781528907156 (Paperback)
ISBN 9781528907163 (Hardback)
ISBN 9781528907170 (Kindle e-book)
ISBN 9781528958493 (ePub e-book)

www.austinmacauley.com

First Published (2019)
Austin Macauley Publishers Ltd
25 Canada Square
Canary Wharf
London
E14 5LQ

Thank you so much to Andy Heather, Paul Prendergast, Sebastian Valencia, Sinead Beverland and Brian Franklin for encouraging me, enlightening me, putting up with me and supporting me through the shady nights, the dark corners, the bars and lapses in concentration. I love you all.

Part 1

I really shouldn't have these feelings of gladiatorial anger, but the people in this place amaze me. If I ask another question and receive a reply of "are you sure?" I am going to explode. Parts of my inner core will propel themselves to the nearest object and not one person would take a blind bit of notice.

Not thirty seconds ago, I asked an engineer if he would make it to site today, to complete the work we have had planned for almost six months and have referenced in several meetings and documents for which his signature adorns the page. His response jars my jaw open, it's as if we have never met or discussed this before, it's as if I just walked in off the street. I am a ghost in my own life.

"You want me there today?" he snorts in my direction, a look of distain etched across the grey pallor of his experienced smoker face. His eyes have sunken into his head, as if they are trying to pull away from what horrors they have seen. Wrinkles and lines so deep, it looks like he has been privy to at least a hundred knife fights in darkened boozers.

I find that my extensive ninja training, coupled with my years of counselling and my meditation mantra's help here. No wait, I have not touched any of that waffly bollocks and I find myself detonating inside. Blood and rage ascend from all over my body and make their way towards my head. I have read American Psycho too many times. I have watched Falling Down too many times. My response should be:

"No mate…It was just a game we had going. I pledge dates to the customer, you agree to them, and I then plan the activities of twelve other workers around you and submit the plans to the whole business. You change your mind or simply cannot be bothered to remember what we have agreed. We

then scrap the plans, chuckle our way through another donut and forget about it...You retarded mass of abortive tissue. Why don't you take yourself off to a massage parlour and find your siblings in the happy endings bin? Your mother must have drunk moonshined battery acid whilst cuckolding her way through a mental asylum, during your gestation period to have spawned such a waste of skin. Why God didn't foresee the mess you would become and push the pregnant whore down a manhole is beyond me. You would have been more use to society if your 'father' would have collected his globular creation in his hand and invented human blu tac, at least then I could have hung the picture of your mother and her first encounter with Billbo the horse on my office wall..."

Instead, I offer a meek "if you could please..." for which I receive no response. Wild and gory images flash in front of my eyes, and I have to shake my head to flush them out. If people realised what I was thinking, they would cart me away to the funny farm. Gradually, I can't help myself and my grey matter stokes to life, the fire of my imagination picking up heat, exploding into a crescendo of hatred.

...Arming myself with a spade and a pickaxe, I wander in early from the empty car park, past a sleeping night guard and take up position behind a filing cabinet near to where some of the engineers I endure on a daily basis sit. Relaxing my breathing, I repeat, "They are worth nothing. It will be a better world without them in it." Closing my eyes, I wait for someone to turn up and my mayhem to commence. It's not long before I hear the door open and footsteps making their way towards me...

"Are you listening to me?" She (Jenny) shoots towards me. Such a lucky man to have a 'boss' like her, I count my blessings on a daily basis to be mentored by someone that has the intelligence and slipperiness of washing up liquid. The mental images retreat, and I try to focus on the surplus human in front of me.

"Of course…" I have no idea, but I play the business lottery game of just saying something that fits the gaps and those around, who are far out of their depth, simply agree, nod or say, "good point".

What business bullshit shall we use today:

Maybe.

We need a meeting.

More information would help.

What's XXXX's view on this.

It's a good starter for ten.

All of them winning hands.

"Well what do you think?" The words highjack my eyes.

I am done!

Right there and then, my resolve is broken and I have no meaningful response to this question, nor an expression to make it go away. There are two choices now, reply with "it's worth considering" or some other rubbish or be a man and explain that I couldn't give a toss. I stare blankly at her, wondering if she has ever been beaten so badly she's urinated blood the following morning. I notice that her moustache needs trimming or removing or shaving, whatever she does to it. Its dark brown and does not match the blonde which is on her head, which in turn makes me think of un-pleasantries downstairs. The way her foundation gathers on each hair almost forces me to retch; resembling something you find from years ago behind the sofa and you have to blow the dust of it to realise what it is.

"Maybe we need a meeting to gather more information, create a starter for ten and get Dean's opinion before we move any further?"

"Good point, I will set up a meeting." Her head drops, and I presume she gets back to her witchcraft or something.

Another meeting of people who just want to get an opinion across; neither agreeing or disagreeing, not for or against, just talking for the sake of talking, costing the company money and growing their pension as they hinder progression. Their mouths turning into the sewerage outlets of a redundant Lithuanian nuclear plant, poisons and pollutants vomited onto those around, causing death and destruction to ideas which the sane people put forward. Normally I sit and clock watch, counting up the people in the room, working out their average salary and how long we have been in the room. This offers me a glimpse of how much money we waste. You shouldn't be allowed in a meeting if you can't answer a request with a Yes or No response. No waffle, no bullshit, no politician avoidance, just a straight yes or no to each and every question posed. In fact, there should be a tax levied at business folk who can't answer straight. Whilst we are at it, then also fine those who ask divisive questions in a bid to keep it all straight.

"Did you fuck this up because you're shit at your job?"

"Yes."

"You get to stay and do it again, without any penalties for being straight."

Or

"Did you fuck this up because you're shit at your job?"

"Well... Peter over there-"

"£20 fine."

"He was supposed-

"£20 fine."

"But, the deadline was-"

"£20 fine."

"Yes... I'm shit."

"You can stay."

This must happen everywhere, right? Surely, I am not the only one begging God above for his intervention and the fire alarm being set off? When you reach this point in your career and you beg for 10 minutes out of the office, to stand on a cold, wet football pitch whilst Stephen, the office bike, calls your name from a register like a clap victim at a GUM clinic, means it's probably time to move on. Or off yourself?

For giggles, I would love to break down and dribble tears during a meeting and explain that my next-door neighbour's, best friend's, auntie's dog sniffed my balls on a fishing trip in south Wales in 1985 and I have never gotten over it. How it haunts me at night, keeps me awake and ruins my sex life. How I blame myself for having such golden shiny sniffable balls. Just to see their reaction. How many would take it seriously, like I was a reject from Jeremy Kyle? What do you call them on Jeremy Kyle? Are they contestants or guests? What do they win? We should gather them all together and take them on a once in a life time trip to a refurbished Auschwitz, and it could be sponsored by British Gas. Now that's prime-time TV BABY!

I look at my diary and think about missing the next meeting and having a 30-minute trip to the bathroom to re-read the dozens of pointless messages I have on my phone. Whoever invented the functionality of text message chains, should be left in a massive cage with a troupe of angry sex starved badgers. It should be filmed and used as press release for next generation technologies – 'get this wrong and the consequence is a badger fisting your ears, whilst his mates eat your genitals' – that would stop me dreaming up anything.

Maybe I should just delete the venomous exchanges between me and my wife, so I couldn't fall deeper into this suicidal swamp pit of hatred. Every time I think I can see or touch a branch to help get me out of it, the tide changes and pulls me away from it, like the whole planet is against me. Desperation consumes me as I think about falling just short of getting out of this pit, another failure to the list. There is nothing I can do as the treacle of depression crawls up my legs and drags me further into its abyss. The helplessness of the imaginary tugging is a constant, unshakable, unfathomable, all too familiar sense of falling until fully submerged into the murky depths of hollowness.

Sometimes I think my soul is on vacation and whilst there, lost its passport.

As we can't get any signal on our phones here, I can't escape and read the Daily Mail online and see what absolute vile garbage they have made up today. I think about punching myself in the face for admitting I read the Mail (*Evil Dead* style), when I tell friends I read the Times, knowing the judgement and ridicule that would come with it.

I am snapped back to reality by her.

"Just sent you an email, can we discuss?" I want her to sneeze, to see if the dust that has doubtlessly gathered within the walrus-like strands of her moustache blows up like the ninja cloud of 70's martial art films.

On a normal day, she looks her age, which I estimate is around 40. On most days, when she hasn't had the time to re-trowel her make up after the gym, she has the appearance of a pensioner's scrotum. Jenny's reputation here is a cross between Stalin and a Playboy bunny kicked out of the mansion for being too provocative. Words are not coarse enough to accurately describe how deeply I despise every sinew in her body. From what I can gather, Jenny has been here for almost a decade, worming her way from department to department. Sleeping, smooching and annoying her way into management. Her desk makes my skin crawl, with empty coffee cups, food wrappers, private reports and gym bags stuffed under there like a discarded corpse. Smelling like one too.

I glance down to my screen as an IM comes in from Seb that reads, "We are all fucked up, we just vary in our degree of honesty and acceptance." Whilst new to the company, he brightens up my days and we send each other horrific, but disguised sentences of putridness to help us through the hours we spend here. I tap out a quick reply, "Only other people are disturbed by my thoughts." His smile is apparent as he beats me quick as a flash with, "Fear and Lusting at Animal Farm – a new novel by Hunter S. Orwell." This guy is good. Before I can get into a heated exchange which would probably lead to a lengthy prison sentence, my ears are boxed.

"In fact, there's no time to read it, let's just discuss it."

Why on Earth do people feel the need to send an email as a discussion point? Bill Gates is to blame. No reason behind it, other than everything computer related I blame on him. He probably sits in his massive house and laughs out loud like a Bond villain at what irreversible damage he has inflicted upon the world. I want to punch him in the ear and ruin him with a yard brush. Maybe I have psychotic tendencies which are suppressed and buried just below the surface, like a drowning soldier under frozen ice, beating his hands on his cell in a final silent show of defiance.

No, sorry I actually have to do some work today. Funnily enough that's why you pay me. Instead of having to read your pathetic, futile, ill written email, which I suspect has little or no value, I would rather blend my balls and sip their remnants through a straw. The fact that you think anyone in the office cares remotely about what you have to say or think makes my eyes water and my heart crumble just a little. If you stood up and climbed over your pit of a desk, flinging yourself through sheet glass windows, no one here would even notice, until the chilly winds got too much for them, their nipples prick up and their breath is visible. Why don't you print off all your ideas, emails, and suggestions etcetera and leave them in the loo where you colleagues can wipe their ass with them? If you printed your ideas on ten-pound notes, you still could not give them away. I am pretty sure that 90% of people here would pay to watch two mutant Chernobyl survivors piss on your face to see if it melted your eyes.

Pride makes its uneasy path to my stomach as I swallow hard and shamefully utter:

"Of course, just grabbing a coffee, can I get you one?"

"Please. That would be great."

I bet it is... You seem to have lost your wallet like Justin Bieber has lost his grasp on reality. I need a second job, just to pay for your coffees. She probably hasn't slept in a year with the amount of caffeine I feed her. People must look at me and think I am your abusive pimp coffee hustler member of staff, feeding your habit and slowly killing your soul, one free cup at a time.

Making my way through the doors I realise that today is a tad more boring than usual and my happy go lucky, sarcastic persona seems to be lacking something. I reach into my pocket to make sure I have the money to buy her a drink, and right there are the laxatives I purchased on the way into the office after three days of blockage.

Snapping the pack, via a cough, I remove one laxative tablet and head down to the canteen to pollute once again. Skipping down the corridor, to pass a little time, draws odd looks from those I pass. I find this adds mystique to my character and generally annoys those who 'work' in the same building as I do. My journey takes me through four different departments, until I find what I am looking for, an empty water dispenser. No one in this office of 2000 people can ever be bothered to change the bottle once it has run out. Like their level of importance will warrant some man-servant to do it for them, as their wavering grasp on reality slips from their fingertips. Stopping the skip, I remove the old empty bottle, setting down beside the dispenser and peel the label off the new one, hoisting it up to shoulder height. Without anyone noticing, I drop the laxative into the top, so is nestles in there and drop the bottle in place, pushing the tablet inside to wait for the first couple of customers. That should make me smile for the next hour and mean that whomever takes that first cup, will be away from their desk for most of the day. Everyone's a winner.

"Thank you, it's been empty for two days now. You're such a love." Her face seems familiar, but my mind draws a blank to who she is or what it is that she does here. Maybe I should set up a meeting and ask her for non-committal opinions on benign subjects, which won't help save the planet. Nameless faces in a faceless organisation, the irony is not lost on me.

"Honestly, it's not a problem… Enjoy!" Partial skip back in my step.

Then it's gone again, before I had the opportunity to enjoy it. Maybe I've not been seen. Maybe.

Bugger, he's coming towards me, I close my eyes and try to disappear. Willing myself to implode and fade into nothingness. Too late, Roy has found me. He is the head of department that does something, which generally no one understands, but I am sure it's very important work that the company could not survive without. Someone once told me that he used to be quite a strong manager and held a lofty position. Presumably, someone figured him out and pushed him down a bit. So now he is irritated all the time, eyeballing everyone around him and inviting them to 'have a go', he resembles a human Jack Russell, full of piss and bile.

Words summersault from him to me, and I don't have my bucket and spade to pick them up. As he's talking to me, I can feel my eyes start to droop, to slowly pull themselves together. I want to sigh and roll my eyes. Sigh loudly.

IN.

HIS.

FACE.

Holding a hand up towards him, like a petulant teenager full of hormones and covered in Lynx. What would his reaction be if I dropped to the floor, curled up in to the foetal position and wailed like a grieving ghetto grandmother?

Do people still take note of this man? He tries to impose himself on others, tries to scare or intimidate them into submission. He is large, with a bald head, high cheek bones and grey skin from too many cigarettes, like those brothers from Eastenders, but fatter. He even talks like them. Like mature cheese, his accent has a twang of somewhere other than the East end. Like he's fake. Fake Roy. I will scribble that in the gents later. Our toilet walls are a little like Facebook, you write to get a reaction, some likes, maybe even a chain of conversation going. What can I say? We're all human. Just reaching out to make a connection.

"Well… Will you sort it?" He scrunches his nose up, showing a dislike for my stench of regular human.

"Drop it in an email and I can review it later."

"It's not that formal, but when will you review and come back to me?"

"As soon as I have assessed your full requirements from your mail and looked at the available resources, their workload and the business priorities."

"I am back to back and unable to get it all written down, this has to be our priority, don't you agree?"

"Again, once I have it, I can sit down with the adults and give you an informed decision. Like you say, it and you, are far too important to shoot back an answer without giving it the proper consideration it deserves."

As he nods agreement to my rehearsed rhetoric, I try to disconnect the taste of shit from my tongue.

Perhaps I should scream:

"You're the overweight human equivalent of spanner rash, constantly rubbing people up the wrong way, continuing on your voyage of perpetual altercations. The world would be a better place, if like a deflating balloon, the hate and hostility seeped out of you and left a regular sized man. The only battle you should concentrate on, is the lowering of your cholesterol as you resume the search for your genitals under the blubberous expanse of your waist."

I literally have no idea what he has said. He could have asked me to help eBay smuggled children from Afghanistan or to erect a patio with the dead bodies of co-workers used for the footings. Surely, I cannot be the only one like this? Scanning the office, I see the same look on different faces. These examples of the office dead. Humans that have had their ambition, integrity and purpose sucked from them by years of fighting a system which is not umpired. My woken nightmare.

Bored.

Tired.

Unexcited.

Desperate.

Condemned.

On a Monday morning, each of these departments must resemble death row. Their desk space is their prison cell, just with fewer bars, slightly better lighting and a worse canteen. It's as if their fate is sealed, options have been eradicated, choices have perished and once you have scrapped away the surface, their life is already over, and it's now a waiting game to see which disease or accident takes them from this life to the next. The slow burning realisation that they didn't win the lottery at the weekend, and they have another couple of days until they sit glued to the TV watching some has-been actor or radio personality play with their balls on screen, whilst crying inside that this isn't what they hoped for, to end their careers. What is worse, making it and then being forced to climb down the celebrity ladder until you're on a 2:00 pm cooking show on channel 8715 which has a critical mass viewer number of 18, or not making it in the first place and moaning that you never had the chance to be discovered?

The jokers wouldn't know what to do with a lottery win. It seems there are three routes, which have been used over the years, since the robbing bastards started selling crack tickets. One – piss it up the wall in drug filled rampaging parties until its gone, and you end up inside a prison or preferably a looney bin. Two – share it with those you love, who then sell stories to the Mirror about you abusing a hamster at Butlins when you were 6 and you retreat to the Isle of Man to find yourself. Three – you don't give your name or any details, you collect the cash and disappear, hopefully to Vegas where you snort and shag your way to an early disease supported demise.

Corridor conversations, that's what I hate. Basically these are the 'off the record' conversations. Those involved are more often than not, the ones without a backbone or any balls – they want to gossip and infuse others with their repugnant thoughts on those they share coffee with and post Facebook pictures with on a Saturday night. Or the ones who want to stir trouble where it needs not be. They dare not put everything in an email, so they have hushed conversations with likeminded people. It's scandalmongering on a professional level. We should install curtains around our battery-hen-work-desks, so these people can twitch them.

He has annoyed me now, by asking me for something without the official record of an email, and my annoyance is heightened as I haven't listened to a word he's said. This will result in him having more ammunition to shoot my way.

"Have you got that info?" or "You didn't reply, did you?" that's all I need, another run in with Plump Mitchell Jack Russell Gob.

Once I have contaminated myself and my line manager with coffee, I can plan for lunch and sit in my car crying, maddening myself to near suicide, and planning how I get out of this place for good. I wonder what I would have to do to get sacked? Maybe defecating on the floor of the canteen is too much, but there must be some middle ground somewhere. My phone rings and brings me back to life, the screen doesn't help me identify the caller. Unusually the call is answered as my curiosity grows.

"Ronny Franklin?" Bad line, I think it's a man.

"That's me…"

"Could you confirm who your father is please?"

"Can I ask why?"

"We have some news for you sir." American accent.

"Marcus Franklin…"

"And his date of birth?" This feels bad.

"May 5th, 1950."

"Sir, I have some bad news for you…"

I drop the call and replace the phone/hate device back into my pocket, wander around to the canteen and wait in line for slop with the other inmates. People are looking at me and I don't quite know why. Maybe I'm paranoid. Maybe I'm crying. Either way, I try to push the call to the back of my mind, as if it didn't happen, and continue to await my sustenance fate.

The coffee in this place is shocking and overpriced, but I did say I would buy her one before our 'meeting'. It has a consistency of weak gravy that gets served in cheap restaurants to those who don't know any better. The aroma is a mix between an old toaster element and the sole of your average running trainer. If we were on the Apprentice, we could bottle this crap and market it as arid land fertiliser, raping the poor farmers and increasing the chances of another recession. Pigs would turn their noses up at this filth.

"Franklin…"

I turn on my heels and a concrete wall of body odour winds me and almost drops me to my knees.

"Rossdale…" Barely audible as I lose the power of my facial muscles and my bowels turn south, I feel something break loose deep inside and I wonder if I've soiled myself.

Dear Lord – take me now. His caustic pong burns my retinas, and I force back stomach bile as it screams into my mouth and looks for the exit. He is my boss's boss. Before I took on this damn project of delivering some overpriced industrial strength planning tool to his entire department, he used to talk to me twice a year, which my senses were particularly happy with. Now, it's almost daily and my features have sent me to Coventry, they ignore my calls and slag me off on a social media product that I am not friends with.

"I need to talk to you about the inadequacy of the tools you have recently supplied my team. They simply cannot get the task complete, with what you have given us."

"How so?" If I gave your team a chisel and a claw hammer, you couldn't get inside an Easter Egg, you imbecilic self-abuser.

"It's so complicated, the training materials you provided do not give sufficient information, most of the team are unable to get into the system, the auto generation of passwords is inadequate – they spend hours trying to get new ones, just so they can get in."

"They all attended the training sessions I put on?"

"Of course, projects permitting of course, it's about priorities."

"I did run them three times and chased up those who missed the course because of their workload. That's each of the 12 courses."

"Perhaps you could run them again?"

As he talks to me, I drift off, I think about what his home life is like - I check his finger for a wedding ring and there is one there wrapped around his smelly little trotter sized finger. What must his wife be like? This guy cannot have showered in a month nor could he in fact fit in the shower. Maybe he has a special one, that a local builder pissed himself creating for an enlarged fee. The government should take away his undergarments and extract the pungent element and manufacture a chemical that could be used in warfare. I imagine him climbing aboard his wife, semi erect penis struggling to emerge from the folds of lardy skin, eventually winning its game of hide of seek with the world. Her nasal hairs long since seared back into nothingness, her sense of smell eroded by years of nicotine and alcohol. I have to bite the inside of my cheek, to stop my fists from clenching and the chubby bashing commencing.

"Can I come back to you?"

An answer is shot my way, but I have lost all interest in whatever he was blathering on about, as my mind clouds over. My gravy coffee is being handed to me and another 8 minutes have been wiped from my diminishing life expectancy. If you were told when your last day on Earth would be, would it change how you behaved today?

"Dude, that stuff will kill you."

"I know, but how else do I stop myself from sleeping at my desk, with all the drudgery I have to endure?"

"Drugs…?"

Paul is my saviour in this place, without him I would have killed everyone on the third floor and lost even more marbles than I have. He arrived about six months ago, just as suicide seemed like my only remaining option and we immediately seemed to hate the world as much as each other. Some of the conversations we have could easily land us with prison time, but the potentials seem to excite us in a way our work does not.

"Managed to kill anyone today?" He sounds sincere.

"Thought about it quite a lot today. I wondered how much damage I could do with a brick."

"Tired" He looks solemn.

"Pick axe handle?"

"Boring" dejected edge to response.

"A child's freshly ripped out arm?"

“Warmer.” His eyes sparkle and I know I have hit a semi high note.

“Biting my way through someone’s spinal cord, wearing a starving pensioner’s ill-fitting dentures and then using their spine as a hammer to bludgeon co-workers to death?”

“And you’re wearing the aforementioned child’s dress?” now he is genuinely excited.

“Shoes…”

“…So close…” holds his hands in victory and then crashes them down on his head in despair/loss.

Lucky no one is in ear shot. Ninety per cent of the people I work with are middle-aged, professional types with 2.4 children, a detached house and a lack of urgency or imagination – your quintessential middle-laners. If one of them overheard us, there would be a full-on observation team from the Met on us within the hour, a tasks force impregnating our homes with recording devices and someone opening my subscription to Razzle and checking for Ricin.

“Busy day?” I try and break off and steer us back to somewhere close to normality.

“Not as bad as yours, missed two meetings, argued with a supplier, played hide and seek with a couple of engineers. Wife divorced you yet?”

“She’s trying to work out the financial benefits of divorcing me against killing me off.”

“You want me to whack her?”

“Give me a week to figure it out.”

“Your funeral, buddy.”

“That’s not booked yet.” Although it was a possibility.

“You want me to come around and pleasure her? She might leave you alone for a while?”

“That’s why we bought pets…”

“Wrong, on so many levels. As much as I enjoy pulling your life apart, I have a meeting to miss.”

Quizzically he looks at me, takes a pen and starts to scribble, mimicking an artist holding up their brush. Once finished, he hands me a post-it note, which has a child-like drawing of a flaccid penis on it and the words “Not to scale, looks like your mum's". This is as cheery as today will get for me, I will miss him.

As I walk past the lady, who I couldn't pin a name to, she is stood at the water machine with a pained look on her face, half bent over the bottle, looking at her own shoes, taking deep breathes open mouthed. Offering a smile and a nod of the head, my energy is too low to even begin to like what I have done to her. But, internal self-five for sending someone a little closer to the edge.

Resisting the urge to throw the coffee over her when I get back to my desk, Jenny looks more hassled than ever when I get back and as usual snatches the coffee without a thank you. Oh, how I wish I could have taken the pain of dipping my cock in the gravy before handing it to her.

"Can you please just read that email and let me have your thoughts, we have no time for pissing around on this, and the business requires an answer."

You my dear, require a throat punch.

Opening up my emails, I delete hers without reading it and mouth the words 'fuck you bitch' out of sight, and with little dignity. Self-loathing score = 10.

"What are you coming back as?" Seb brings me back to life with an IM.

"I presume you mean in the next life."

"No… tomorrow you aged cock face. I'm losing patience with your under developed grey matter."

"Hopefully a porn star's genitals."

"Cher's balls."

"How old do you think she is now? 108? 109 maybe?"

"In all honesty, I think she passed on several years ago now, and her unknown illegitimate son flayed her, wears her skin and has a Death Becomes Her potion, he uses every day."

"Are you available for public speaking? I think you could have a decent career as an after-dinner speaker. Not for all types, maybe the WI or various knitting clubs"

"I have other important things to do, must dash. Don't top yourself, just yet – we've only just met."

The rest of the day passes without incident and I manage to get some of my reports complete and out into the ether, never to be read. Resembling a fox, I say my goodbyes/enjoy your nights/don't fiddle with cats and head over to the car park. I remember when I smoked, I was much happier, at least I was clawing the end of my life ever closer, and I was in control. People don't really understand self-harming, they think it's a cry for help. But I do cry for help and self-harm, so go figure. Maybe it was always going to be this way? Maybe life was penned from the start. The same people think that self-harming is what teenagers do with blunt knifes in their bedrooms, it has such a greater presence and all of us at one time or another have indulged. Most people can't draw the correlation between drinking, smoking, taking drugs and self-harm. A gambler friend of mine once told me that it was not the potential to win, which drew him to the betting shop, but the chance of losing it and having to deal with the consequences that peaked his interest.

Easing the car out of its space, I drive to the gates and offer a semi sincere good evening to the guard. I don't hate him, it's more like a mild displeasure that he is breathing. He is not as bad as the socially repugnant mind terrorists that work on my floor, but he could be. I stop the car just around the corner from work where there is a little layby most people don't know about, dangerous to get out of, but far enough from the main road so that I can't be seen.

The tears form and explode out of my eyes, flooding my vision and racing to escape my face as it seems even they can't stand me. My shoulders attempt to dislodge themselves from their sockets, as I uncontrollably shake my way through the sobs. The wailing shocks even me, and I bang my head against the steering wheel in frustration, not knowing what else I can do. Inside the pain, the hurt, the frustration and anger collide throughout the day, it's only when I get outside that the volcano erupts. My ears hurt as I wail and shout and curse and hate.

The car door opens, and I almost fall out. There is a man stood in front of me and I can't make out his face through the stinging embarrassment of my tears.

"You OK pal?"

"She died…" I let go of a memory

Reaching, scratching and searching for the door handle, my hand inadvertently makes its way towards his crotch, as I complete my mission and fall out of the car. I am now on my knees, in a layby, crying my eyes out with my hands round the balls of a strange man. The comedy of my depression starts to kick into fifth gear, as he bats away my hands, mutters something homophobic and returns from whence he came. Dropping on my behind, tears are removed by my sleeve and laughter pours from me, twisting itself free from deep inside my body and finding no audience as it dances through the air spasmodically. An onlooker would be genuinely confused, if not scared, if they happened across me right now.

Is he crying, should I help?

Is he retarded and laughing at the traffic?

Maybe he will head-butt an oncoming 18-wheeler?

Maybe he has the courage and has given up?

As I sit on the tarmac on the roadside, traffic now and then making its way past me, people driving on to happy homes and loved ones who care, I realise I have no reason to be alive anymore. I can no longer think of a person whose eyes brighten when I walk in a room, whose handshake and "good morning" are genuine, whose kisses are warm with excitement. Suicide, as an option, has been there or thereabouts for some time now. It's slender hand resting itself on my shoulder in the dark with increasing frequency, tempting me to accept its handshake.

Whilst every person has suspicions and lapses in confidence, I raised my game recently and started checking up on my wife. With a heavy stone shaped heart, I read through text messages and emails as she showered or pottered around in another room. Sickness rose within me and overtook the blood in my veins, forcing a stammer in my heart and a quickening of breath. My fears were true, there was someone else. Thankfully, not someone I knew, but it seems someone she now knew very well. Intimately. Passionately. Very much like we use to know each other. Those memories have been washed away by strong liquor, late night arguments and a cold spare room with no comfort blanket. The only saving grace for me is that her new significant other is female. Not that I am masculine enough to offer more anger and hate towards another man that I carry for myself. Her final kick in the balls, was sweet, even for her.

My phone is on the seat of the car and with new found energy, I pick myself up, dust myself off and get back in the car to have a look at how many missed calls I have today. Yesterday was 11, the day before only 4, which I must admit did upset me more than I thought. Sixteen today, all the same number, the same US number. Maybe I should get it over with and talk to them. Maybe I should get online and research the most painless way of hitting my restart button/light switch/engine cut off. My fingers hover and then make their way towards the photos on my phone. In a scene reminiscent of Bruce Campbell, one hand fights the other and the gallery is not open, not today. Today is anniversary number two. Two whole years have gone by and it still feels like yesterday, every time I close my eyes in a quiet room, I can reply the conversations of that day, as if they were on film. Time heels everything, they said. They are dead wrong. All time has done is make everything bleaker and me more resentful.

730 days.

17,520 hours.

Mirrors should be banned I think, as I look up and despise the reflection that stares back at me. Normal people wouldn't be able to understand the feeling of despising your own reflection. Looking deep into the cold, deadness of my eyes, thoughts develop in my mind, maybe today is the right day. I start the car and decide it's time to go home and discontinue the monotonous charade that is my life.

Stopping at the garage on the way, I get out and showcase the mud, gravel and dirt that has collected on me – as usual no one takes a blind bit of notice. Internal planning takes over, and I fill the car with petrol and wonder how long it takes to gas yourself from the exhaust fumes.

"Just petrol?" The unnamed male attendant is gruff and annoyed as I enter to pay

"Yes, thank you."

"We have some pocket torches available today." He points towards something yellow and black on the counter top. It resembled a miniature dildo.

"O.M.G. Seriously? Wow, that's just what I need. I have honestly been searching the whole day for one of those, the miles I have walked from shop to shop, you wouldn't believe it. Couldn't find one in M&S, Farmfoods didn't have one, nor did Zara. How utterly and pathetically stupid of me not to try the exorbitantly expensive petrol station for an illumination tool. How did you end up here? Were you thrown out of stage school?"

"Alright mate, I was only trying to help." His eyes look hurt.

Throwing £60 on the counter, next to the torches, I turn and run at full speed from the shop and back to the car. Blood which has risen from my heart, which is running at full pace, to my cheeks, feels as if it is going to burst out of my ears and eyes and mouth and forehead. For the first time in my life, my thoughts leaked into my vocal cords and my consciousness didn't force my lips closed. I am euphoric. And sweating. And smiling.

Entering the car, swift movements turn the ignition on and my feet mimic Mansell as I hotfoot it out of there and resume my commute, cackling like a mad old woman, the outside world blurs past me without a flicker of recognition. All of a sudden, I am hot, perspiring, leaking happiness from each and every pore. People talk about a rollercoaster of emotions. They should try being a manic depressive, it's the longest and scariest rollercoaster you can imagine. But it's free and the queues are to die for.

A red light halts my progress and my brakes glide me to the line. I shouldn't have done that. It was not his fault. What I have done is acted in a way towards him, which I loathe from others when they act that way to me. But it did feel good. It felt right, that I should say what I am feeling inside. Rather than the words eroding my interior, they are now a bad memory for him. Is it true that you have to repent your sins when you get past this life? Wonder if a church would let me in to repent? I suspect they would need to keep me in for a while if I ever got there. Not that I am a religious type, I just wonder what it is all about and if you feel a little lighter after pouring out your darkest secrets to a complete stranger. It certainly sounds cathartic.

Our driveway used to be my switch off point, before I entered the house all feelings of depressive guilt and overwhelming anxiety would be shelved, leaving them in the car for the start of tomorrow when I would put them back on like a well-worn tie. Now-a-days, I am unable to shed the poison that flows through me and I suck it as deep as it will go, but it's still there, still with me, just bubbling beneath the surface and ready to pounce at any minute.

The new neighbour is on her drive. Her name is Angie, but we call her Aging, as she acts well under her years. We fell out a while ago, the standard argument over hedges or bushes or something trivial, and we now have a mutual hatred for one another. We have managed this without actually knowing anything about the other. Pretending to be on my phone, I laugh into it as I exit the car, trying to look preoccupied and distant.

"What kind of bloke are you with a laugh like that? Not exactly, manly, are you? You're not for me love." A dragon snort of laughter leaves her as she turns.

"Whooooaaaa!" she turns back, with what she thought was her sexy smile, unfortunately my mood had oiled.

"I apologise, we haven't really met before. That's a little bit harsh coming from a 'lady' who dresses down by 20 years, but let's assess the situation. You're pseudo strong and judging by the bags collected around your eyes, which have been prematurely brought about by at least a few blokes dumping their laundry at your door, my guess would be that you are a worrier. Someone who stays awake all night, replaying the cockups of your life. I'm thinking a husband or maybe two, have come and gone. Your clothing, whilst clean and respectable is cheap, suggesting a lower than average income, poor vocational choices and in turn limited intelligence or a pile of debts left by an aforementioned spouse. I would wager that you frequently go to cheap pubs like our horrendous local 'The Local'. That tells me that you have struggled in the past with the social environment of a decent place like a wine bar or non-'Local', where you were probably dismissed by the men who patronise them, as sub-standard or second rate goods. Now you take your chances at the aforementioned, because you think you're better than them and that you are in control. My approximation is that most Sundays you wake up with a deep sagging hatred for yourself, laughing it off and offering them breakfast, whilst semi forced to offer fellatio, tears stinging your eyes as they complete their business and run off to tell their mates how easy you were. Week nights are spent analysing the soaps, with a hurtful realisation that your depressive collage of ruin, is a far bleaker existence than the likes of Dot Cotton. If you were as strong as you repeatedly told yourself in the mirror after the horror of your Sundays, then suicide would have been completed years ago. But I have a sneaking suspicion that you have failed at this, like you have at most everything else in life. On the plus side for you, I have heard that portraying the life of a working girl on Craigslist, whilst drunken, would more than likely end up putting you in a mutually agreeable position with a psychopath, thus bringing about your demise and saving face when at the Pearly Gates. Good day."

Today is different. I stand tall and stride into the house, confident and at ease with everything, even a smirk has broken out on my face like a tear in a life boat. There was little point waiting for a response, it would have been feeble and misjudged like almost everything in her life. She may even phone up one of her Saturday night folk and plead with him to deliver retribution for her in exchange for sweaty and emotionless acts, but I am past caring. At least one of us is smiling.

Shit.

Bags.

Packed bags. In the hallway.

Begging me to trip up on them.

An unavoidable obstacle course.

Bags containing marriage.

And hope.

And dreams.

And topped with despair.

My smirk shrivels up and hides somewhere dark.

"Ronny, we need to talk." Strike one, I volunteer for the 8 count, I know the next shot is going to hurt.

"Can we give it a miss tonight and whack a film on?" my humour is lost on my wife, not for the first time. Our eyes meet, but I don't want them to.

"I'm leaving tonight and have arranged for the rest of my stuff to be picked up later on."

"Is this the right time to divide the DVD's? I promise I won't haggle over the rom-coms?"

"Why can't you take this seriously? We have tried to have this conversation for months, years even." I can taste my stomach as I watch her face contort with despair.

"Two years... To the day." The ref should take a point away from me, for a low blow. Immediately, I want to rewind and start again, it's not her fault.

"Why can't you just get on with life, it's been two bloody years!"

Two bloody years reverberates in my ears, then fades to a silence neither of us seem comfortable with. Our eyes find other targets around the room, as the seconds drag on. We blame each other, without laying blame. We hurt each other, whilst hurting ourselves. Forcing half a smile, I surrender my palms in the air and she nods her approval.

"Let's not make this worse than it needs to be." My offer is laid out before us.

"OK."

"Who will be picking your stuff up?" curious more than aggrieved.

"Does it matter?" Nothing lasts forever it seems. Her facial display may as well have been a punch to the testicles. Tom Cruise once said, in a film, "Everything ends badly, otherwise it wouldn't end."

She is still attractive, still looks after herself and knows how much of an effort to make. It's not a great surprise that she has found someone else and moved on. Part of me is still in that room from two years ago, rotting away day by day, refusing to let myself out. Her hair is tied back today, business-like and purposeful, dark brown and well looked after. Recently I have noticed that she has regained everything and more of what she lost of herself, two years ago. Maybe I gave up parts of me and she took them in. Maybe I haven't noticed enough. Maybe does not count at this point. It's no good blaming the fart for the smell, after eating the curry.

When we first met, she had a smile that could stop the rain. Sometimes at work, I counted the hours until our next date. There was an energy inside her that wasn't human, she could keep going and going. Nothing got her down, nothing was too much trouble. Whenever something bad happened, it was her I would go to and pretty soon everything would be OK.

Walking past her, I wish my ears would close over and I didn't have to hear her anymore. I wish it was two years ago and I had dealt with the situation, the questions, the problems, the issues all back then. But I didn't. It's now and now I have no excuses. The woman I love is ending our marriage and walking out the door to someone else. My inner rage is picking up and I need to escape this by either walking out of here or by magic – but it seems my wand is broken and any rabbits hiding up my sleeves died some time ago. This has been coming and we have been wordlessly fighting about it.

Surprisingly, the rage quickly begins to subside, and a strange feeling washes over me, like a soft, calm, warm wave, starting at my head and working its way down my body, picking up negative energy on the way and depositing it at my feet. Subconsciously I look down at them to confirm that a repulsive yellow energy hasn't pooled itself down there. Something clicks into place, a penny drops, a revelation, call it what you will, something happened inside my head.

With an easy smile, I look at her for one last time and remember how good she made me feel for many years. Never again will I set my tired eyes on her frame. Never again will I get the opportunity to protect her in some small, nameless way. Never again will I get the opportunity to apologise.

"I guess you're right and it's for the best, you get yourself off and when you are ready, just drop me a text to say when you want to come over and pick the rest of your stuff up. My only request is that it is you that picks it up and not someone else. I will not stand in your way and cause a fuss and I will support you in any way I can. I want this to be as simple and as easy as we can both make it."

The sincerity is real. When we break it all down, there is no hatred between us, it's just what lingers after the love dies. Why should I stand in her way and stop her from living, it's what she wants to do and it's what I love about her, just wanting to get on with it. I don't own her, so why am I angry with her?

Me on the other hand, I am very different, I just want to arrive at the end. Looking back, it's like buying a book and reading the synopsis on the back and the last page. The book is going to be a great read, with a shitty ending – but you still buy the book because you know you will enjoy the journey it takes you on. Even if the last stop of that journey is the cesspit of a bunny abattoir, during a hurricane.

A moment passes between us, she considers what I have just said and then forces a tiny weak smile.

"Thank you, I appreciate that. I will get off, leave you be. Drop you a text tomorrow and then pop round to collect a few bits? We can sit down then and start to divide stuff, if you like?"

"That sounds like the best thing we can do."

Not even a backwards glance as she walks off and closes the door on us. No goodbye hug. No tears. No remorse. Our life together is over in a heartbeat. There could have been a thank you or an admission of appreciation for what we achieved. Nothing. A void opens up, yet the room seems smaller. There is no time to ponder the what ifs and maybes. Her life now follows a different trail. Looking up towards the ceiling, my knowing smile broadens as I release the weight built up in my lungs.

My mind is now made up and I have to move quickly to make sure I complete everything I need to, before the alarm of my life goes off. Moving quickly up the stairs, I grab 3 envelopes and a new pad from the office, making sure I use the expensive pen I was given as a birthday gift last year. I hold it in my hands and read the engraving:

"Your words encourage me to be better."

She may want to rethink that soon. I go into the bathroom, open the cabinet and reach for two packs of pain killers which were prescribed recently when I had put my back out. Two of these would have me asleep for 12 solid hours, I wonder what a pack would do?

Taking two at a time, I make the whole flight of stairs in 4 easy movements and catch the door handle in my right hand on the last move. Flinging it open, I bounce over to the car, pull open its door and quickly start her up, pressing the garage remote and moving it inside. I am back within the safe walls of the house before anyone on our street has had the chance to even see me or what I am up to. I close and lock the front door and double my foot pace to get back to the paper, pen and the dining table.

Letter 1:

Mum,

It's been tough for you, no one can deny that. But much tougher for me than anyone really knows. Empathy never was high on our common list of limited traits. All the times I wished you were there, you never made it. All the invites I sent for you to see me, were left without a reply. Why? What did I do that hurt you so badly?

For whatever I did to you, I am sorry. Maybe it's too late and the words don't mean much to you. You missed the dance at my wedding, I shed a tear when you weren't there. Maybe we can meet up again somewhere and have a dance. The tears have flowed and I don't have any left for you, but why did we lose touch for all these years? I won't leave here, hating you or anyone else, hopefully my apologies reach you.

Anger has left me, but I hope the last few years of your life aren't the hardest.

RF.

Letter 2:

Joe,

I wish we would have been closer. Although we lived in each other's pockets for so long, I never really knew you and that saddens me. Regardless of your size and strength, I always thought I could take you on in a fight. Granted, I would have to sneak up on you as you slept, and use a bat to break your head, but under those circumstances, I reckon I had a chance.

I will miss your belly laugh and the fact you could eat two packs of biscuits, one after the other. You were the only person I ever called a friend and meant it with all my being. Remember when we drank too much and tried to play football? You turned up with a clinking bag, I had a half-eaten pizza and we barely made it on to the pitch. You sat down in the centre circle and tried, in vain, to put your socks on for almost 20 minutes, before we were asked never to return.

We have lost touch recently, as I have battled the past two years, and I can't blame you for keeping your distance, it must have been hard after the birth of your daughter. Don't for a second think this has anything to do with you or our friendship. Finally, I am able to make my choices for my reasons.

When you have a pee from now on, think of me stood next to you, asking why yours is so small.

RF

Letter 3:

Dad,

As I am writing this, I can't help but feel it will never reach you.

I could write the same things here that I have just written in Mum's, but where's the fun in that? Over and throughout our turbulent relationship, we had so many challenging discussions and arguments that it's difficult to know if there is anything left unsaid between us which is worth saying. You always encouraged me to put my points across and argue your way through anything, but never allowed me to speak. This was aimed at building my character and only now do I realise what you mean. You feel much better about yourself if you just get it off your chest.

You liked a good argument and having the last word, drawing out arguments over years and years, until the other person cracked and gave up. With that in mind I thought I would write to you.

DO ONE!

RF

I write Joe's address on the front of one of the envelopes and Mum and Dad's on the other two, plus Private and Confidential. There are several other people I could write to, but my enthusiasm for it is fading as quickly as it took hold, and my momentum has swung from saying goodbye to the event itself. Picking up my work phone, I have decided it would be unprofessional not to record an informative answer machine message for anyone who would like to leave a voicemail.

"Hi, you're through to Ronny Franklin, apologies, I can't answer your call right now because I am swallowing a gazillion pills and washing them down with a pint of vodka. Ten to one this voicemail is still playing a month after my corpse is stinking out the street and letters are clogging up my doorstep. And that is how much your custom means to us. If I didn't write you a letter before I forced my own demise, it's because you meant less to me than a dose of diarrhoea. Which is exactly what you'll get if you drink the water in our offices. Have a nice day now."

This last line is delivered in a broad, appalling Southern American accent, with just a nod to the owners of the company who command from out there. Irony is lost on most people, so this is another part of my legacy that will loiter without a laugh.

Last and certainly not least, I thought I should email my boss, detailing the reasons why her lack of empathy over the last two years has helped my mental comet reach this late stage of its trajectory. I could pour my heart and soul onto the page, ripping myself to pieces in the process and unearthing further torment and animosity, leaving the reader with a tear in her eye and lump in her throat. Then I start to think more about the reader, the partially retarded bag of excrement that has ruined my life with her inability to think, act or rationalise as a human. She is a disease. A parasitic management relic from an era we hoped had died out. The simple fact is, the point of my letter/email would be overlooked and the response would be an attempt to stamp her authority some more, pointing out grammatical errors and the need to separate the sentences more. In fact, she would probably call for a meeting to discuss, asking why I thought illuminating her Blackberry mail light, out of office hours, was appropriate. Inviting senior management as the undertone of my suicide note was aggressive. An agenda would be set and a link to the current HR guidelines included, so I could familiarise myself with its contents prior to being bored to death. My thoughts are turned to a late-night telephone call and voicemail, just as I enter the other world, my last breath would be heard by her, as a wheeze that carries my final words on earth…"I wish you had died before me, so I could have taken a dump on your headstone."

The letters are placed into the envelopes and sealed, dropped on top of my Blackberry and positioned on the sideboard, so whoever comes in to find me, finds them first. It's done. Everything I needed to do is now done. This must be how someone with a normal life feels when they finish work on a Friday! All my chores are done and now I can kill myself, so I don't have to do it next week…

I pull the hose out of the back garden and drag it into the garage, remembering seeing the fat bloke on Full Monty, sitting in his car and tasting those fumes. This will help. Grabbing a full roll of green and yellow electrical tape from the drawers in there, I position the hose in the middle of the exhaust pipe and start to tape it in place, using about half the roll. Using a pair of pipe snips, I cut the hose down in size, so it's just long enough to fit into the rear driver's side window, which I have cracked open an inch. I use the remainder of the tape to close out any gaps on the window and stand back to admire my handiwork. Will this actually work or is this just something you see in films? I chuckle to myself, that for the past three months, I have been badgered to fix the cable on the kettle, the electrical tape was bought for that task and now it will be used on my final task. And the kettle is still broken.

Climbing into the driver's seat, I have pills, vodka and a CD from the great Jay Z. One song is needed for this. The only song which still to this day, brings me to tears. December 4th. The human leftovers I used to share an office with, would have gasped and gone into brain spasm at the mere thought of listening to such an artist. Shaking on the floor, clutching at their throat as they death rattled Jaaaaayy ZZzeeeee, before their forever unseeing eyes rolled backwards and rested on the grey matter which carried minimal traffic. His work came up in conversation once, in the canteen. They chuckled their way through undeveloped and inane reviews of his music. Trying to be the good guy and expand their limitations, I pointed out that he had more platinum albums that Elvis and equal to the Beatles. Instead of a retort, they ran like the kids of

Columbine, screaming as if chased by Freddie and still none the wiser. Running back to their 80's soft rock and the safety of rockin' all over this God forsaken world.

The engine struggles, coughs, farts and fights its way to start, the fumes entering the car, as I pop all the pills from both packs into my hands. This is the right thing to do. Hurling them as far down my throat as I can and raising the metallic tasting cheap vodka, I swallow as much as my eyes will let me. The concoction has a Lego consistency which erodes my trachea as it enters my stomach. Tears fill my eyes, retches fill my mouth, pain fills my head and coughs fill the car. Using the steering wheel and the gearstick, I crack my knuckles and shake my head, hoping to remove some of the evil I have passing through my system. I belch, sneeze, choke and cry at the same time, fully focused on not losing my lunch and spilling my deadly dinner.

It wasn't just the fact that we had split up. Looking back, there was the divorced parents, never ending custody battles, the endless line up of partners and step parents, the lack of clothes and the subsequent abuse thrown by peers, the miserable nights alone, the malnutrition and lack of brain power brought on by a poor diet which conceived a depression long in the making. All that before my teens and long before the events of two years ago.

Minutes pass.

Everything is slowing down and has a haze around it. My eyelids close and my head bobs to a beat that is not there, thoughts drip, rather than flow. Jay Z kicks in, the whirling sample, the drums and his mother saying a few words, before I hear the ones that make me weep like a child:

"Now I'm just scratching the surface cause what's buried under there was a kid torn apart once his pop disappeared.
I went to school, got good grades, could behave when I wanted.
But I had demons deep inside that were raised when confronted – hold on
Now all the teachers couldn't reach me
And my momma couldn't beat me

Hard enough to match the pain of my pop not seeing me,
SO, with that distain in my membrane
Got on my pimp game
FUCK THE WORLD!
My defence came."

Another huge swig from the bottle and I recline the seat to almost flat, I close my eyes and find memories I buried years before.

I'm 9 or 10 years old and I'm in my mother's bedroom, very late at night/early in the morning and its summer. It's hot. I have eczema, and nothing can stop me scratching at my invisible monsters. For the last couple of hours, I have been laying on the floor, scratching my back against the rough, cheap carpet, sitting cross legged in front of the open freezer and fanning myself with a tea trowel trying to ease the pain. Not for the first time, I even sprayed half a can of woman's deodorant onto the infected parts, but it only stops the burning for a few seconds and offers its own burning in return.

It's been three days since I saw her last, since I ate, since I left the house, since terror started, since I used up all of my tears. On the underside of the windowsill in her bedroom, I use my thumb nail to indent the aged gloss with how many days. This isn't the longest one, not by far. Standing at the window, with the curtains open, I listen for cars and with everyone that I hear approaching, my spirits rise, and expectation grows. Disappointment beats me down, like the schoolyard bully, laughing in my face for being so stupid. I open the window and crane my neck, so I can see further down the road, challenging my eyes to beat my ears and find her first. Another car, another hope, another disappointment.

Hunger pains, exhaustion, distress, anger and fear reduce me to a shadow of myself – a cardboard cut-out of a happy child. Looking at myself in the long mirror, she uses to check her clothes before she goes out, I notice that my ribs are visible, just the bottom three on each side. Also, my skin is starting to look grey, apart from around my eyes where it's almost black and the scratch patches are getting bigger at my elbows.

I have no energy, not enough to even stand and I fall to the floor, resembling a pair of unwanted jeans, crumpling around themselves. I don't want this to go on, how can I stop this from happening? Could I take a breath, a deep one and wish hard enough for it to be my last? There are no tears left, but the crying grimace contorts my face, mocking me for the lack of tears, a deep sense of failure overwhelms me – hits me as a reflection from the broken mirror. Maybe I could go to sleep and dream forever. A happy dream, where I don't have to wake up anymore.

My eyes are closing, the exhaust fumes have made the interior of the car extremely warm, but it's a pleasant warmth, which is mixing with the pills and the booze. Blinks seem to take a minute or two to pass and my head filled with glue. In my hurry, I have forgotten to leave a letter for my wife – was that intentional? Half of me wants to stop the clock and go write one, say sorry, pour myself onto the pages and beg for her forgiveness, offering sincere explanations and opening up about why I was this way. The other half wants her to wonder why for the rest of her life. For my final scene in this play of a life, to torment her and keep her awake at night, wondering just how big a part she played in this final act.

My self-induced time machine has brought me back to my youth and for the final time, I just want to sleep and dream and never wake up. Tiredness takes full hold and the fight is slipping away. It's taken around half an hour for me to end my life. But in reality, it's taken two years. Exactly.

Part 2

It's bright and my eyes need a few seconds to adjust and take everything in. Without noticing my head shakes from side to side, as if trying to rid itself of the contents. The building in front of the car looks familiar. If I were a computer, the egg timer would be busy, as I search the broken cells in my brain for an answer. Many times before, my eyes have caught the black windows reflecting absolutely nothing back. The red brick work was probably classed as a design revolution, when it was conceived by the poorly paid architect, who was hanging on to his university dream of recreating the world with their moniker etched all over it. Is this my office? It could be, but there is something different about it. Something cleaner. Not cleaner. Purer. I can't put my finger on it and my thoughts unable to take form like smoke in a breeze.

What did I do last night? I feel uninhabited – like part of my essence took a vacation.

There are no other cars or people milling about the place, yet I don't feel alone. Nor do I feel that people are watching me or stood next to me. Confusion leaks out of my pores, yet I am at ease with myself, with a distinct lack of anxiety or pressure. In autopilot, I exit the car and make my way over to the building, which is only 20 steps or so from where I have managed to park. This can't be my office, there would be a million people in there by now, and I would have to park in a different postcode, jogging in to avoid the looks from those who share my misery at work. Driven by an inner force which it seems, always existed. Stopping in front of the doors, I raise my head and try to take in the whole building, seeing if I can see the top, but I can't. It goes on forever. Well, not forever, that would be impossible. Maybe I am standing too close and my angles are all wrong.

The silver metal door is surprisingly lighter than it looks, or I have developed super human strength overnight. Turning back, I watch it silently return to its closed position and I'm inside of a huge atrium, which is warm, bright, unspoilt and almost surgical.

"Next."

Turning to face the where the voice came from, I see a mammoth, well, erm, reception desk? Only it's not a reception desk, it's something far different, and I can't form enough words to do it justice. This desk is bigger than the room, only that's not possible, but it looks like it is. Imagine walking into Dr Who's Tardis and seeing a football pitch. There are people behind it, going about their business, moving what looks like paperwork, faxes if you are of a certain age.

"Next!"

My feet are glued, this thing before me is too large to comprehend, how did they get it through the front door? How many men had to sweat through the early morning sun to get it up the stairs. They were probably thinking "If only I had concentrated more at school, I wouldn't be here." or "Why was I abused?" or "Drugs got me here, they will get me out of it."

"There are no drugs here Sir, now I presume you are next, so please step forward."

Who is she talking to? Do I have an office here? I'm starving, where's the canteen?

"Sir! Step forward and I can answer most, but certainly not all, of your questions."

She has no face. There is *a face*, but not what I would normally expect to see. It projects light, it's bright, like a torch beam – although not direct – but a lot of light. But there are no features. No definition around the nose, no crumpled forehead from years of disagreement and no lips to convey thoughts.

Then the voice or the tone of her voice… it's different. Not robotic, but not human. Not monosyllabic, but without feeling or emotion, just words trickling out and eventually joining with others to create a sentence.

My gob is smacked, and I stumble forward, apprehensive and defensive at the same time, heavy feet dragging and forcing themselves forward towards unfamiliar surroundings and an uncertain future.

"Do you have a route in mind?"

"A what?"

"A route, which way did you think you would go?"

"Do you mean who do I bat for?"

"No. This is not sport."

"Certainly not one I have played before."

"You're not helping."

"Should I be here?"

"You're here, you have a choice."

"Home?"

"That's not one of the options."

"Can I see a menu?"

"This is not a restaurant."

"Good, I would never choose this; the waiters do not seem qualified. I doubt there is even a sommelier."

"Soon there will be other people."

"Can I eat with them?"

"Do you know them, from before?"

"Before what?"

"Here…"

"The ring road?"

"Life."

"I'm not following…"

"No… you're not."

My mouth has not opened, and I have completed a conversation with a flash of light on a body. Although not a body I have come across before. Sweat should be forming on my head, I am not used to direct and conscious discussions with people I have never encountered.

"You will be fine. Just step forward, give me your name and I can help."

"Why do you need my name if you can hear my thoughts?"

"Fine… I am only trying to help you and ensure you get to the correct route."

"Where do you think I should go?"

"Turn to your right, can you see the stairs?"

"Yes," I add awkwardly.

"Walk towards those stairs and right in front of them is a glass door, enter that door. Don't be tempted to use the stairs to go either up or down, just use the door in front of you. Someone will help you in there."

Maybe I actually said thank you or at least thought it, but it seemed this conversation was over now. In robotic fashion and devoid of thought, I turn, lock my eyes on the door mentioned, and will my feet to wade through the air treacle and take me there. My feet make no sound as they shuffle along. I glance down to make sure they are touching the floor and I am not sliding around like a Moon Walker. In fact, there are no sounds now, not from me, not from the building or the torch thingy. Nothing. When I get to the door and raise my hand, I realise that I am holding my breath, or not breathing at all. The hands of anxiety are wrapped around my little yellow adrenal glands, both being pulsed by them to ensure maximum secretion of catecholamine's.

The door opens into a room, which is bright and airy, with a dozen or so seats, all facing into an imaginary circle and no windows. How can it be so bright without any windows and no visible lights? There is a board at the foot of the circle, just a simple white board, with words, large bold words on it, but I can't make them out. People are sitting on the chairs, one by one they realise I am standing there, and they shift in their seats, so they can see me clearly. Whatever was happening has now stopped, and I am the centre of their circle.

One of them stands up. A woman. She seems to be the leader. She has features, I can make out lines and points in her face, a nose here, an ear there, all normal. Pretty, but not amazing. She is talking and, thank the lord, not stopping to acknowledge my thoughts. She holds out her hand, it points in my direction:

“As we have a newbie in the room today, I will start again. Please join us, help yourself to a seat and don’t feel like you have to contribute until you are ready. We start each session with an overview of yourself, so the group understand where you are coming from. Each person tells their story and then we can start.”

Expectation. Eyes on me. As I am not sure what on earth is going on, the best thing I can do is to try and stop these eyes and reduce that expectation by joining them. The air treacle is thicker here than it was outside, it feels like my feet are nailed to the floor and I need all my strength to pull them up. Despite it only being a few steps towards the empty seat, I seem to be taking forever. Initially I felt their stares were investigating me, but as I meet a couple of them they soften, and I even attract a smile from one.

“I am happy to start. My route here started at the age of twelve, when my father broke all the rules, well the rules that all other adults seem to follow. But we don’t have to talk about it here. Back there, my name was China, I think my parents used to smoke a lot, or they were Bowie fans. I seem to have forgotten everything else before I was twelve, as I don’t really have many memories.

There was a boy at school, Adam, who was different to everyone else. He didn’t ignore me or make fun of me, at first it was just a smile, then more and more until he said he loved me. Just like Daddy used to, but in a much different way.

So… after a long time of just being close, we started to mess around a bit more and did some things that maybe we shouldn’t have. We fell in love, but he said we had to hide it because of my age. People would say I was just a kid, he would get into trouble, but he knew me differently from everyone else. We drifted away from everyone and before long, he offered me something to smoke. It was bliss, we would stay in bed all day together, we were so close.

That was until the time some of his new friends showed up and he wanted me to love them too. Said it would help us get by. I smoked more and cared less. Seems my young heart couldn't take it after a while and I have been here, every day, ever since. Which seems like forever now."

"Thank you China. Charlie?"

What the fuck? She's a child. Can't be any more than sixteen, but something about her screams older. Her eyes avert my gaze and she is back looking at the floor.

"Charlie, nice to meet you newbie – don't worry, we can grab your name later.

I made it into the 27 club by meticulous planning and exquisite execution. It was one hell of a birthday gift to myself and I could not wait to get inducted . Over there, before, I watched from a distance, never really getting involved, never really fitting in, the face that no one recognised. Could have been modelled on that Brett Easton Ellis character in the Rules of Attraction. Most people managed to forget about me, whilst in the middle of a conversation with me. I guess I never managed to forge myself into one of their memories. Unluckily though, my family money meant I never had to try, never needed to work and occupied myself with living through my music.

From an early age, basically from when I could read about my heroes, I knew when I would go, it was just about how. Don't mind it here really, you get used to it."

"I'm glad you're used to it Charlie, but the idea is to get out – to find your route."

Where is here? Who are these people? I don't want to say anything. Can they hear me like the torch receptionist? That route again, what does that mean?

Hello…Seems not.

"I'm Mitchell, been here way too long and would like to get through it and leave as soon as possible. I don't say much, cus I don't want to. I'm here and that's pretty much all you need to know."

"Thanks. Bob?"

"Bob here, quite a few sessions in here now and I am still learning the ropes. Before here, I drank too much and, in the end, it became the end."

"Shit… I remember that line in Leaving Las Vegas where Nick Cage says, 'I'm not sure if my wife left me because I started drinking or I started drinking cus my wife left me.'"

"Not one I've seen I'm afraid Mitchell. Think I am still coming to grips with this place and why I am here and what the meaning of it all is. Guess I have many regrets and things I should have done. Did I mean to get here? I don't know."

Bob shuffles the feet he now gazes upon and for some reason, I want to rush over and give him a cuddle. Odd, because I don't really ever remember wanting to cuddle anyone.

"Well that's everyone. I am the coordinator of the group and it's my job to get you talking. There are no rules, there are no topics that are not allowed and the idea behind them is for you to be open and to enjoy this discovery. Newbie, you might want to intro yourself at the next session, but no pressure to, so let's take a break."

They break and seem to know where they are going, I look towards them and see Mitchell's shadowy eyes booming in my direction and I follow him. Where? I have no idea.

"It's retarded mate, no one knows why we are here or how to get out. I have seen loads come and go, god knows how they get out – one day they are spilling their guts about all kinds of depressive shit and then you never see them again. We just meet up and talk and talk and talk. If you want the $2 tour, I can't give that to you. All I know is, over here they have a sensory room, who knows what that means, I haven't been to it. Some people come back from it in a right mess, so whatever it is, I ain't buying. Fill your boots though, as some people never come back from it."

"Are we…dead?"

"Of course…what did you do to get here?"

"I can't quite remember. I was in my garage…"

"You topped yourself, you idiot, we all did. Some might not think it, but we did, that's why we are here. Each person has to figure out how they get out of here though. I have seen them all mate, the abused, the haters, the accidents, the planners, the remorseful, the glad, all of them. And don't think you will get any help off her, she barely says a word and 'encourages' us to speak."

His forefinger and middle finger push the air as he says the word encourages and his eyes roll to show his displeasure. I stop walking, as the blow hits me.

"I killed myself?"

"Yeah… it takes a while, but it all comes back to you soon. Then it gets hard, because you start to feel guilty and think about those who you left behind. But it doesn't matter, cus you're here and nothing really happens from this point forward. Walk over that way and there is a view, it's the only one I have found, but it helps me think. We call it the gallery"

He points over to what you would call a viewing platform , a massive window-like object. Stunned and wordless, I make my way over and try to fathom what the hell is going on here and how on earth I get out of it. What is weird, is that I don't feel anything inside, other than mild confusion. No anger, no pain. Not the all-encompassing alarm and panic that you'd assume comes as standard when you find yourself in a situation like this.

"If I was you mate, I would stick here for the day, you won't get bothered. Try and sort your head out."

He left, I stayed, and my lips curled over, as my head spun. The gallery was blank, nothing there at all. It was similar to the thing Tom Cruise used in Minority Report, but with nothing on it. Mitchell seemed OK here, not puzzled, not dismayed, just here. As he walked away, I tried to think about what had happened to him, as he seemed the elusive one, in terms of his past. Although he was clothed, we were all wearing the same, so it was difficult to place an era or timeframe on his existence. The way he spoke wasn't particularly from any period of time I could make out. Glancing back, I now picked out images on the screen in front of me. They were of a child, walking in a garden, nappy on, creases of chub around the joints, smile on the face. It may have been me.

"I'm China…"

Snapping back from whatever caught my eye, her beauty caught it this time – just her face. Massive blue eyes, thin eyebrows, high cheek bones and clear skin, topped with Side-Show-Bob style blonde curls and a smile which made you feel good about the world. In a club, she would be the one dancing and enjoying herself, whilst I watched on feeling unsure and overwhelmingly unconfident.

"Hello…"

"Do you have a name, or should I make one up for you?"

"Sorry… Sorry, my name is Ronny, it's great to meet you."

"Is it?"

"I'm not sure, really."

"After a few sessions, you will get used to this place and before long it's just another day."

"Can I take your word on that?"

"You can have my guarantee on that!"

She became a lighthouse and the room her warning zone, such was the brightness of her smile. Immediately my mood grew, and everything seemed like it was going to be OK.

"China?"

She stopped and looked back at me, smile still firmly affixed.

"It is great to meet you Ronny…"

She winked and skipped back like a teenage day dream. How old am I? Seriously, I need to get a grip. This place represents God's waiting room. I feel like I am awaiting judgement from a jury of my peers. Hang on, is this purgatory? There is a group of people, who all seem to have left their lives under a cloud, we are all dead. What if this is the place where it's decided if you go up or down?

I have a new sensation, one which I thought had been persecuted out of me, many moons ago. My own smile broadens as the realisation hits me and my conclusions are formed. I am excited. There is no point in waiting, I may as well just join in and see what happens.

Each person took up a chair and discussion ensued, but I am not sure if I was listening, thinking, planning or even in the room with them. This may have gone on for hours, for a few minutes, I don't know. Time just seemed to trickle away as we entered the third or fourth or fifth session. Glued. To be honest it could still be the first. My lens is covered in Vaseline and the edges are blurred.

"Newbie… Are you ready?" A gentle smile and genuine warmth as I am invited to say my piece.

"Yep… This is my first day, I was sent here by God on a mission to uncover the truth. When I first met him, at a Tesco in Southampton, I was initially concerned by his lack of facial hair. Ever picture and portrait I had ever seen, he had a strong beard, a hipster beard, but in a real-life face to face situation, he didn't. Well, he asked me to infiltrate this very group and to get the back-ground information of the coordinator, find out what she did before this role."

Collectively they smirked but did not laugh. Maybe this line had been used before. Maybe all lines had been used before. Maybe I had been here before. Maybe this was not happening and it's all in my mind. My messed up, warped little mind that didn't mean much to anyone, not even me.

"Do you really want to know what I did before I got here?" There was a seriousness to her now, my challenging commentary and intended puns had not hit the right spot. Do I get a yellow card or something for being facetious?

Her features now became clear, the lines were great in numbers, she wasn't aged, but she seemed to carry the weight of the world on her shoulders. Once, in the past, years before, she would have been beautiful. Her hair looked strong and long, but the colour had been sucked from it, leaving just white. There was nothing behind her eyes or if there was, I couldn't make it out. No colour, no passion, just a driverless cockpit.

"The rest of the group have heard this, but as you asked, here goes.

My final day started normally, well as normally as it could. At the time I resided in a hospital, Rykes Hall or RHPU or short. Gone were the memories of how I managed to find myself there, but the emotional pain I felt that day is still present. Depression infested my being the way termites take over a tree. A poison to the mind, administered by another and nurtured by my inability to find a vaccine.

By the end of my time on Earth and life as a human, it gripped my whole body like a vice. Hunger was a distant relative, the frame of my body weak and fragile, bones jutting in abnormal directions and a paled skin tone begging for nourishment. I remember feeling calm. I remember letting go. I remember the final seconds. I remember no longer being scared.

For some reason, I didn't have to attend the meetings you find yourself in today. HE gave me a job straight away. I trawled from delivery room, to car, to ambulance, to waiting area, to bathing pool, to anywhere the baby decided to show its head and force their way into a brave new world. There was not a place on the earth that a child couldn't be born, and I had seen most of them first hand, witnessed the tears, the pain, the happiness and the jubilation of that emergence.

When I first started this 'role' I tried to keep count of the good experiences, the ones where hope existed and the future was lengthy and anticipated. Quite quickly the realisation that the bad experiences far outweighed the good ones, settled in and my personal hell was born – excuse the pun.

Occasionally when things were going badly in the DR (that's what the hospital staff call the delivery room), I would try and help, radiating any and all positivity that I had left, offering whatever soul was left in me and trying to bring a swift and happy conclusion to the proceedings. Kissing the foreheads of those who lives would be something to behold, they would become someone.

At first, those who died straight away bothered me greatly. An intense desire within me, yearned for them to be given a chance, to try and make it outside of those walls. Witnessing several thousand still births soon cleared my emotions, and deadened me to what I was a part of. The dejection and pain in the mother and those who she chose to have around her, washed over without drama. I became immune.

Every time a new one burst their lungs and joined the earth, HE would send me a number. That number would be the number of days that human would spend on the Earth until their time was up. Some were only a few days, some were much longer, some carried a normal lifespan, some were tomorrow. My job was to present that number to the new life and bestow on them, their death age. This was my punishment – my crime unspoken and forgotten.

Death day, as I call my last day on Earth, was not the day I ended my life. It was the day I gave up and stopped trying to live. When I entered 'purgatory', I thought there was an option, a gate, a decision to be made. There wasn't. Instead of a detailed interview, in front of a panel of 'better' people, with a swift and decisive conclusion, I was moved and started work without comment.

My touch was toxic, breaking down, poisoning and eradicating those who come into contact with me. Forever. For eternity, I brought about the eventual demise of tiny humans. Their first and sometimes last experience was me. There is no eternal burning of my flesh, no fiery pit where I am forced to endure for the rest of time.

My resolve was broken, I was empty, and HE came to me and I was moved on, here with you people."

Whilst the group bowed their heads in unison, I became aware of the freedom I enjoyed now.

"Any medical with that? A pension scheme perhaps?" Calm faced.

"You can carry on with your performance, for as long as you like. We are not going anywhere."

"But there must be a way out of here." Statement, not a question.

"Have any of you asked much since you have been here? Watched anyone leave? Noticed anything?"

"Why do you think you are you here?" the question attached itself to a certain amount of pity.

"Calm down, sister. Let's see what these guys have to say."

A few groans, but a collective nothing. Mitchell was first to offer thoughts:

"I have seen so many people come and go."

"Me too. But I have never asked them anything." China seems happy to have a new topic of discussion or is just happy not to be talking about her. Or Daddy. Or Adam. Or his friends.

Bob and Charlie were quiet and looked exhausted.

After several minutes of discussion, it became apparent that not one of them had done a thing to work out how to get out of dodge. Nor had anyone noticed if others had come and gone. It's like they had given up when they got here. Wait. They gave up before they got here.

"Back there, enough was enough. I couldn't take it anymore. Life was heading in the opposite direction for me and I wasn't sure if I wanted to see it park at the end. I suppose I chose to do myself in, so I made sure I had one more decision in me. Did any of you think there was a place like this?"

Nothing back. It was like talking to the dead. Life had literally been sucked out of them and there was confusion all around. I decided to take it up a notch.

"Have any of you asked how to get out of here?"

Similar blank page.

"Coordinator – how do we get out of here?"

"You need to find the suitable route."

"That's not really helping now, sensible answer?"

"I'm not able to tell you how, each person is different and there is no standard route. You need to look inside yourself and find the route."

"China, do you open up much here?"

"Not really, I don't want to say the wrong thing or make a fool out of myself."

"Seriously? There is nothing anyone can do to harm you here, strap on a pair and say what you feel." I am the host on the Jeremy Kyle afterlife special.

"Bob, how are you feeling? Do you or have you seen anything like a route?"

"Ha… I'm OK, I guess. Suppose I am wondering how things are, back there."

"Why?" If someone doesn't challenge me soon, I will implode.

"Because I have left people, things, stuff that I should have done."

"What does that matter now?"

"Well… it… I… well. I guess it doesn't matter anymore."

"Correct! There is literally no going back, there is no point in worrying about it."

"What should I do then?"

"Figure out the route, by the sounds of it." I was starting to enjoy this.

"Mitchell, you look so down. How long have you need here?"

"Too long mate," dejected and distant.

"What were you like back there? Friendly, chatty, polite, human?"

"Guess I was quiet."

"Not much of a talker?" I hit the sarcasm wall and found a few bricks to add to it.

"Not really."

"Why?" This is painful.

"Who wants to listen to me anyway?"

"I do Mitchell. Tell me something you never told anyone before."

"I don't know. There's nothing really." head bowed, starring at his feet.

"I am genuinely interested to know something that you never thought you would be able to say. Anything. Something. Please? We don't know you, it's much easier to speak to strangers."

He took a deep breath and raised his head, eyes locked on to me.

"I'm gay."

"You dress pretty smart and it looks like you took care of yourself, I can see it. You never told anyone? Not a parent, a friend, no one?"

"No chance, people would never speak to me again."

"What makes you think that?"

"Dad always called people, blokes you know, puffter, queer, all that."

"What about friends?"

"Just guys at work, I worked in a factory in the north of England, there ain't too many gay people there."

"Were you married?"

"Yeah and I loved Michelle, I really did. I tried for ages, you know, to make it right with her. Like it was in my head or something. It was me not her."

"You miss her now?"

"Yeah," sadness rolled down his face, but colour had come back to it.

"So you just hid the way you felt, all of your life?" This was heart breaking and my sarcasm got on a bus, leaving us to talk. It was just me and him now and I wanted him to break down those walls, those barriers, and be open. Be gay. Be himself and not have to worry.

"Pretty much. I watched things you know, films and that. Once I even went to a club in London and watched, but I knew I wanted to be with other blokes. Didn't have the bottle to do anything, it wouldn't have been right to cheat on her. It wasn't her, it was me."

"If you could go back, would you do things differently?" I shifted closed to him, the circle collapsed, and it was me and him.

"Suppose so. Although I loved her, guess it wasn't right to marry her you know. I hope now that I am gone, she finds someone new. I really do, you know."

"Don't answer if you don't want to, but did you take your life because you couldn't hide the way you felt anymore?" I held his hand in mine, although he tried to pull it away, I persisted and offered him comfort.

"Suppose I did. I felt like a fake, a phony, a fraud. Inside, it ate away at me, little by little every day. Guess I sunk into a kind of depression you know. I had nowhere to go, no one to talk to."

"Who knows what's right or wrong…come here pal."

Raising myself from the chair, I held open my arms. Shock forced him to almost flinch out of the way, but he gently rose too and met me in an embrace that old family members give each other at the twice a decade wedding.

"No one is here to judge Mitchell, judgement is something the living try and hand out." Sobbing left him and found a home with me.

"But that's just you, other people would have judged me. It's fine saying that now and realising it now, but it's too late. I am gone. Now I am here, and I can't fucking get out of here. This is almost as miserable as it was back there." Anger stuck him, but not anger for being there, anger that he did not take this stance before. Before he got here.

"It's OK now. Nothing can hurt you. No one will judge you. You need to be you."

We released the grip we had on each other and I saw a different look in his eyes. A softer gaze. His shoulders kept their position instead of dropping. He held his head up.

We all broke off and retreated into different corners to think about what just happened. I was starting to search my remaining brain cells to think about Purgatory and what (if anything) I had read about it. Looking back, back to school, I think I remember something in RE about this being an intolerable place where you had to atone for your sins.

Being gay wasn't a sin, was it?

Surely not when faced with the big man, he wouldn't be able to say that, no chance. The world has enough shit in it, without us condemning those who choose a partner of the same gender. And when you look at it, this place was actually quite snazzy, in a surgically clean/OCD dream, kind of way. It was certainly not intolerable. I could stay here a while, but certainly not forever.

I realised that I was buzzing, I hadn't felt this alive, since I was… alive. My head screamed, let's get back in there and open these guys up, I am convinced I can help them all in some way, shape or form. On reflection, maybe I shouldn't have ripped into the coordinator like that when I first walked in, but I don't feel the need to apologise to her, probably had much worse spat in her direction than what this failed rag of a human could offer. There is an overwhelming desire to strike up conversation, I need to ask lots more questions and see what the rules are here.

Are there boundaries in here? There must be. Maybe I am presuming too much and there are no boundaries, I can literally ask what I want and try to help where I want. What's the worst that could happen? I am already dead. Making my way over to see what problems I can cause, a confident smile adorns my face, and I am pretty sure it shines for all to see.

Everyone is here. Wait. I can't see him. We need to continue where we left off. But he is not there. Mitchell has gone.

"Where's Mitchell?" I ask the group, but they just look at one another and the search for an answer draws a blank. The coordinator is sat away from us a little, I turn, and our eyes meet, she has a shit-eating smirk on her face, like she knows exactly what is going on and we are all on the outside of the programme.

"He found his route."

"What?"

"He is no longer with us." She looks away from me, like we have reached this end of this to and fro.

"Why? Where? Up or down… figuratively speaking?"

"That's not a question I can help you with, all we need to know if that he identified his route and took it."

It was because of me. Well, because of the questions I had asked. That line of questioning, those simple few words, those admissions, his admissions, his peace. Mitchell had solved his own riddle. He answered the ticking bomb at the back of his head, which led to a door being opened for him. Finally, that man was at peace. Is that what we need to do? Admit the things we never had the chance to back there?

"May I ask a question or two please?" The nod of her head was my green traffic light, I depressed the accelerator.

"Of course you can, I will always try and answer. If I can't, it's not because I don't want to, I just can't."

"Can I presume that there are three conclusions to all of this? Let's say Eastwood style good (up), bad (down) and the ugly (stay here forever)?"

"Not sure I follow the Eastwood reference, but in a roundabout kind of way, you are correct." She should play poker; her face was steel and her chips guarded.

"Can I get a look at them? You know like a snippet, a trailer of it? I honestly don't mind if it's a Green or Red Band version."

"Most of what you say, I understand. But sometimes, you really do lose me with what I assume is your sense of humour – or what you would class as your sense of humour. Most of it depends on the route you take and like we agreed earlier, each person is different and as such, undecided. Maybe we could look at the bad, as you put it."

"Now we are talking! Let's do it!" I had lived through enough, I could take it, what could they possibly have for me that was worse than I had already experienced?

"The easiest way is for you to walk over to the viewing gallery and step inside. That's actually what it is there for. Each person has their own experience in there and it is based on things I can't describe or offer explanation for."

If I had a heartbeat, I would have made it over inside one of them. This was going to be interesting; I would be able to see into the dark side. Into Hell. Exciting. Think I skipped over there and went in through the main door. It is vast inside and dome shaped. At the front was what can only be described as a cinema screen. A huge cinema screen. It was curved, almost upon itself, it took up most of the dome. There was a theme park back then, called Alton Towers, it was open in the 90's. They had something similar back then, the 360-degree cinema or something like that. I make my way inside and the curve closes behind me, the cinema screen now covers its entire inside, I am now inside the cinema. It is me.

There is residual light inside and it turns from a multitude of greys into molten black. The colours seem to be turning in on themselves, eventually turning darker until they reach an absolute black. Deep black. Cold black. As I look around, I have no idea where I came in, which is the front or which is the back. It's just darkness everywhere, eating away and consuming any light. More importantly, I don't know how I would get out if I needed to.

My limbs are starting to feel heavier. In fact, they are very heavy now and I am being forced to take a knee like a wounded boxer. All of a sudden, I am sitting down and the substantial weight of the air around me constricts me to a prone position on the floor, I am sucked into place by gravity, unable to move a muscle. In front of me, a picture is forming, something from the past. I can make out objects, white objects against the bleak background and objects are becoming clearer. Breathing has become difficult, as my throat narrows and pressure is forced onto the front of my rib cage, restricting me to shallow intakes of air. It's hot. A hospital bed is visible now, right in front of me, my wife lies on the bed, soaked in sweat and wearing a gown which carries as much sweat as it does blood. She is cloaked in misery, it radiates from her, the look on her face, I have seen this before. I have been here before. This is my past.

Someone else is in the room; dressed is green scrubs and their face covered by a mask, looking in my direction. He is holding his arm out to me, mouthing something that I don't want to hear. Her scream breaks the silence and hits me. It pierces the air, breaks the matter around it and makes me shudder, my head repeatedly shakes as I try to pull away from whatever is there. He repeats the words in my direction, but looking away from my eyes:

"I'm sorry… There is nothing more I can do, she was not strong enough and she didn't make it I'm afraid."

Words leave him and force their way into me. The screams are continual, over and over. The reverberation of his words echoes and repeats louder and louder still, piercing my ears and drilling into my brain. Her tormented face bulges and expands to ten times its normal size, cold wet flesh against my face. My ears hurt as the decibel level rises further still, now I am screaming. The sounds melt into a cauldron and the words hit my organs, each one is a car slamming into me, mashing organs, ruining me. An invisible boxer is punching the words into my face. Intense heat from the screams, the words, the punches, her face against mine. Breathing is almost impossible, I gulp at air and try in vain to get some inside of me, to try and relieve the pressure in my head and against my body. I want to claw away at my neck and allow air in via an alternate route, but my arms won't move, I am imprisoned by torment and personal suffering. My world is collapsing in on me, my daughter is dead, and I can't do anything. Pressure. I am under water, far under water and in pain. I'm dying. She's dying. She's dead. I couldn't save her. I failed. My genes didn't allow her to live. It's my fault.

It spits me out, I am discarded like human waste, hitting the floor with my head, banging my fist against it, howling in grief, screaming with hate, crying like a wounded child, thrashing to free myself from the pain, the noise, the anguish, the angst – which is no longer there. For a few minutes I stay still and compose myself, lower my breathing and try to calm myself down.

That was two years ago. That was when this started. That was when my journey to the end, began for me. I didn't want to go back, ever. I never wanted to relive those moments, again. That day was when my body stopped pumping oxygenated blood. Instead self-loathing and a distaste for my situation seeped into my bloodstream via a deadened heart and polluted me from the inside. I never thought about it, I never questioned it. Despite my wife trying as best she could, it was buried deep inside me. Us. Me.

Like a fish out of water, I was marooned in front of her, arms not knowing what to do, legs cemented to the floor, but chest rising and falling in chaotic fashion as I cast my eyes over it and towards the coordinators legs. Looking down at me, any feelings she might have for me and the expression its teamed with, is on its permanent vacation, lapping up sunshine and cocktails instead of contaminating its countryside. I ache. I am in pain. Mental pain. My body has failed me, again.

"Did you see what you wanted to see?"

"I… Missed… The… End… Credits… What… time's… The… Next… Showing?" Coughing up soul after each syllable and chewing on my failures bile.

"Did your sense of humour ever get you in trouble back there?" I am pretty sure a smirk welcomes the words as they as hastily thrown towards me, but I can't open my eyes for fear of what I might see this time.

"No not really, not in the common sense of it. If you want my suggestion on increasing the viewing figures, I think if you moved towards having one of those half time ice cream vendors in there, attendances would shoot way up."

Struggling like a man twice my age, gingerly I raise my body into an abnormal yoga pose and take some deep breaths. The still birth of my daughter ruined me. Watching her mum, my wife crack and break like that changed something inside me. I pushed all of those thoughts, feelings and emotions deep inside and tried to block them out. It was the worst thing I had ever been through. Physical pain heals, quickly if you're that kind of person. The emotional stuff builds up and up, the smallest of things adds weight to what's there until it bursts, explodes and the only residual presence is destruction. It could be personal destruction or something else, someone else, something there and you stop it being so. At some point it will come to a crescendo, the hurt volcanoes out of you and usually takes out something around you.

She'll be better off without me there. No messy divorce. A new chance for her. I have done the right thing. I don't not want to go to the bad side, that pit of personal hell, I couldn't take that. I deserve better. Barring the last couple of days, I have led a reasonable life, nothing that should stop me at the pearly gates.

I gulp a massive noisy intake and gasp at the same time (it's something reminiscent of B movie acting), people around me stop and notice. The group is there and they look on inquisitively, awaiting the next move. I know now. I know how to get out of here. It's not just about opening up, it's about coming to terms with what you have done. Hiding feelings, not dealing with stuff, it's all unfinished business.

Finish the business and get out of here. That's what Mitchell did, he admitted to not feeling he could live as he wanted. It's not about sinning. He fought against telling people what he was inside, which brought about his untimely demise, albeit at his own hands. When he finally accepted what he was, said the words outright and wasn't bothered by people's reactions, he got out of here. Excellent – move to plan B.

I could see the stairs and there was an internal sensation to follow my instincts and have a closer look. Maybe I could try one of the routes and speak inside, just to see what's on the other side. I could come back surely? Should I be hesitating? If it's meant to be, I would have just walked over there and skipped a few steps to… to whatever is there.

Wait…

Wait a minute. She said something about the route was not decided. That means it's not just about coming to terms, admission or saying things aloud. What if you admit the wrong things? That could mean you end up 'down' so to speak. What if you had buried a crime deep inside and this place was the only way you opened up and admitted it. Having that secret with you at all times, would drive you to suicide, ultimately the good and bad of society would end up here in the same room. Talking to each other. Who in there was good? And who was bad? What if by admitting that I should have made things better, earlier, I get judged as a bad person and find my way 'down'? Mitchell was a good person, he must have gone 'up'.

I don't just want to get out of here and find out what's next, I want to help these guys through it all and out the other side. Let's get back in and see what we can do.

Like a pensioner after a fall, I raise my beaten body and realise that people are still looking at me, awaiting the next move after my gasp.

"Sorry guys, I just realised that the gallery was not going to show Top Gear and I had forgotten to record it, before popping over here."

Honestly, comedy is ruined on these people, it's like they have more pressing matters to deal with. I take myself off, into a corner to lick my wounds and some thinking time. I don't want to leave. I don't want to end up in a hippy field, singing songs and laughing at the breeze. Nor, do I want to end up in a fiery hell, with looped repeats of 'the worst day of your life' shown on an un-flickering cinema screen at a decibel level, humans shouldn't be anywhere near.

Life, as I experienced it, was pretty shocking and I didn't cope with it well. Inside I was a different person. Confident, quick witted, fast on the draw with an answer or opinion for everything. On the outside, I was the opposite, pretty much a failure. What if I could make a difference here?

What if this was my chance to right some wrongs, to be a better person, to be good at something? She holds the key. The coordinator was close by, so I tore my bruised ego from its resting spot and went over to her.

"Is there an apprenticeship for what you do? Can I log on and whack some details in, start the ball rolling? I am happy to go down the old YTS route, it's not about the money or prestige of role, I just want to get into a career. Can you imagine if this conversation came up with your career officer at school? I think I would have ended up at the funny farm."

"You want to do what I do? This is not a job."

"I think I could help these people to reach their destination, to find their route and the way out of here."

"Maybe you are missing the point, what if they don't want to find it?"

Puzzlement etched itself on my face, rather than words forming on my tongue.

"Did you know where your destination was when you got here? Do you in fact, know where that is now?"

Further puzzlement and chin scratching. Maybe I hadn't figured it all out.

"What do you know about these people?"

"Nothing. But isn't that the point? I get to know them, and they figure out what's gone wrong and then click they find their route, to coin your phase?"

"Try and answer my question, what do you know about these people?"

“Apart from what was said in group therapy, not a great deal. This isn’t One Flew Over the Cuckoo’s Nest, I am not Mr Nicholson, surely the idea is to get them in, sort them out, get them out?”

“I think that just highlights how little you appreciate what we are trying to do.”

“Do you have a mission statement, a set of values, something I could read? I did ask for an apprenticeship, I am prepared to start at the bottom. Well, not down there, in the middle, here, you know what I mean.”

“Much like with your life over there, there isn’t a list of things to do, a path to follow, a map or anything like that. There are no rules, no mission, no statements.”

“So what is the aim of this place?”

“To support people. To listen. To wait.”

“Wait for what?”

“Whatever they need. Think about what we have discussed. Take things on board. Try and come to terms with a few things and watch what’s going on around you. That’s all the advice I can give you and the only piece I am prepared to offer.”

What did I know about these people? Nothing really. A few sentences when I got here, hardly opened up to me have they. What did they want? I didn’t know. I am one of these people now. What did I want? What did I know about me? Again, nothing really – I had spent the last couple of years in a stalemate, my world had stopped spinning. Throughout that entire period, I buried thoughts, resisted conversation, hid feelings and avoided the rest of the world.

The group were making their way back over to the meeting spot, so I slowly headed over and I listened. And listened some more. I offered nothing back to them, when it was my time to speak I passed on it and let someone else pick up the reigns. When the group broke, I questioned myself. I tore myself back to basics, asking the difficult questions, figuring out some answers. When I could get her alone, I asked questions of the coordinator. Probing and learning all the time.

Over time, I had mind novels for all of them. I rehearsed their stories when we broke and listened to the conversations they were having outside of the group. My lack of interaction didn't raise much more than a curled lip and a heightened eyebrow, they seemed used to me being quiet, much like the outside world, I became part of the backdrop. After time, they did not ask me to join in, I did not need to pass up the invitation, they simply moved on to the next person and I shifted my gaze ready for more words from the next person.

"Was what I saw in the gallery supposed to be hell?"

"Who says there is a hell?"

"I see where you're taking this. There isn't a hell. There isn't a heaven. There are a couple of options for you to take. Let's say up or down, just for mapping purposes. People have this pre-conceived idea of what heaven and hell is, would you agree?"

I noticed the coordinator shift her stance, thinking, not wanting to give it all away.

"You are people. If you say so, I have to take it from you that is correct."

"This is what I have figured out. For years and years, well actually two, since my daughter died, I didn't want to be on earth, slash, alive anymore. What stopped me? Hell, that's what. Having read books and seen films, the thought, actually the nightmare that would be there stopped me. If you have ever read Chuck Palahniuk's Damned, you would see where I was."

The blank expression and lack of response made me think she wasn't quite up on modern literature back on Earth. I carried on with my point.

"The thing is, I had witnessed hell before I got here. I didn't have to die to see it, I lived it. Hell is the worst day of your life, exaggerated, inflated and intensified by 100. What I saw in the gallery, was that day, that life ending day in the hospital, where everything went wrong. But with heat, and anger, and pollution and, and, and…"

"What's your point?"

“Maybe this is my heaven…Your job is my heaven. Dealing with people, helping them come to terms, understanding them and what they have been through, getting them to a point where they can move on to theirs.”

“It’s an interesting point.”

Although she never smiled, or laughed, or showed what we would call emotion, I could see something change in her. Almost unrecognisable, but recently all I had done was watch these people, minor changes were like tidal waves to me. The slightest change in the organic make up was a tsunami size, about turn.

“When I first got here, the receptionist thingy, person, asked me which route I was following and I didn’t know what she was on about. I am a little slow, you may have figured that out.”

Almost a nob of the head, I was really getting somewhere now.

“I could have used the stairs and gone up or down, or I could have ended up in this room with you lot and all these questions and meetings. Honestly, have a look down there and see an AA meeting or a Grievance meeting, they rock in comparison. Answer me one question, please, if I took the stairs, I wouldn’t have ended up in a room of people, I would have found my route?”

“You would have followed your route.”

“One more question please. Did you use the stairs, when you got here?”

There was a slight pause and a flicker of thought.

“No.”

“In your opinion, could I do your job?”

“It’s not a job, it’s a duty.”

“Could I preform your duties at your level?”

“It’s not my decision.”

“Give me a little sugar please! In your opinion as master and commander of this group of people who have gathered here, could I do the same thing you are?”

“You could listen, as you have been doing. My duty here is to listen, offer any words that might help. Like I have said, it's not a job, there is no set of actions or pre-arranged list of deliverables."

"Can I ask them some questions in the next session?"

"We are here to help each other, to listen, to talk."

"I don't want these guys to leave, I want them to feel comfortable."

She turned and walked away from me, towards the others who were gathering for what felt like the ten thousandth time, to talk about the same things they had talked about for the one millionth time. I was going to bump my way in, offer my story and let them make the next move.

"Would you mind if I spoke? If I told you my story in full?"

Some shakes of the head, some intrigue and one who seemed to have forgotten me. Here goes…

"I was born into a semi affluent family, higher working class you could say. My father worked away in construction, he would regularly be away Monday to Friday each week. That left me with my mum, my half-brother and half-sister. Throughout the week, I mainly waited for him to come home. Looking back, I never felt I fit in with the rest of them. My mum had been married before, giving birth to my siblings, but the spousal abuse intensified, until she left him and took the kids with her. After my parents met, it was not long before she was carrying me. My father had recently lost his son to leukaemia. Looking back and making wild assumptions, I think they had me to fill a void. When he came home, I would spend pretty much all of the weekend with him tidying up his van, going to his office, kicking a ball and walking our dog, who was a present to the family the day I was born. Those weekends lasted forever and the weekdays took forever to yield another weekend.

Whilst I cannot remember any bad times growing up, I remember lots of good times. Until my father did not come home one weekend. He stayed in London with someone else and eventually, three months or so later, on the 18th March 1989, I overheard Mum on the phone saying that he was with another woman and would be divorcing her and we were moving. Some place much worse than I was used to, via social services to a council estate

I retreated to my room emotionally, physically, figuratively and I changed. The sharp wit and humour he encouraged me to show, died. My smile eroded and was replaced by a self-induced exile. On my own, away from everyone else, nothing could hurt me. Looking back, the pain of that time has never seeped out, never been discussed, not even to my wife, not even to myself.

He promised to see me every week. The first time he picked me up, it was my birthday and he brought me a blue Walkman, music was our thing and it was an amazing present. My first memories are of me and him singing Eagles songs, and he also had a copy of it as a second gift. It was thoughtful. But in other ways, it was the start of a set of irrational behaviours that would tarnish my life.

He would always be there at a weekend and I could not wait. We had such good times, we joked and nothing was ever serious, as a kid, you remember that. I never wanted it to end or go away and now it had. Every week turned into every fortnight, which turned into now and again. Eventually I hit 15, Mum had gone, I was sleeping on peoples floors and I hadn't seen him in a while. He moved to America I heard, but we never spoke again.

That Walkman was a big gift for someone that lived on a council estate and a single parent home. I wrapped that thing in rags and paper, in a box under my bed, scared that if I took it out and enjoyed it, it would break and not work again. During one of our many late-night house moves, it was left behind, I was broken. A year to the day after he left, our dog died.

This became a theme throughout my life, I would buy things that I really wanted and put them away, never to be used or even see the light of day. I guess I did the same with my emotions. Even my wife. I hid everything from her in the end. Scared of pushing her away, losing her.

When she was pregnant, I could not wait for our child to be with us. I could start life all over again. It didn't have to be the way my life was. Anticipation grew as her bump did and pretty soon, our child would be born and at night I went over how I would change. How this new person changed the script, re-wrote the rules for me. I would be re-born as they came into this world.

And then she was still-born. She was born and took a few gulps of air, before her tiny lungs struggled to flex enough for air to be taken in, causing all the other organs to fail. She died in my arms, as my wife struggled to hang on to hers. It happened again. Something I loved and cherished left me. The two years from that day until I got here was me putting off the inevitable. A major part of me died when she did, mine was just a longer, more drawn out death than hers. When I got home two years to the day after that day, my wife was packed up and ready to leave me. That was the final push. The nail in my coffin if you like. I no longer had a reason to carry on.

There are many things I regret, but not really knowing what happened to my father is something that still pains me now. Never going for a pint with him, not once did we erect a tent and cook bacon in the morning on a mountain side, never telling him how much I loved him or just having someone there to fall back on."

All eyes were on me, the entire group sat and looked at me for more words, but I had nothing left. That was everything that was built up inside of me, and no one else knew. Unlike films and TV, there was no standing ovation or clapping of hands, their stories were far worse than mine.

I got up and the group broke away. I took myself off to a corner and faced away from the rest of them unsure what I could do next. It was hard to say those things to people I did not know. Was there anything else in my life that was unfinished? Whilst a weight had been lifted, I still did not feel that was everything. There was still something else I had to do. Deep inside me, I thought my route was right here.

I look back and Bob is walking away, shaking his head. He is leaving us, heading for the stairs, I am intrigued to which way he will go. His trudging steps seem loaded with emotion and almost reluctantly, he finds the stairs and heads down. I want to stop him, to help him, but something halts my movements and forces me to watch.

"Looks like he is off." China stood next to me and I shift my gaze to her.

"And he's going down the stairs." I bow my head as if watching a man head towards the execution chamber, leaving his personal prison and taking his first steps in a new life.

For the first time, I notice another viewing room, on the opposite side. I am pretty sure it was not there before, I would have seen it, I've spent enough time here to see every angle.

"Have you been in either of the viewing rooms?"

"No chance, I saw you and several others come out of there and it was not pretty."

"Out of them both or just the one I went in recently?"

"To be honest, that one over there comes and goes."

Compelled, I leave China and make my way over to the 'new' one, heading into this one it's bright and there are noises. Soft noises, almost music like. They wash over me and make me feel at ease. Dropping down, I sit cross legged on the floor and a kind of calmness eases its way into me. It's now completely white with a single black dot in from of me, which is getting larger.

I start to make out figures, a place, a bed, my wife. Instantly, I want to get up and run, fearing a repeat of what happened earlier, but I fight the urge as something tells me to stay. She has a different look on her face now, not like before, not like I remember. Many people are around her, but not rushing, unruffled and controlled this time. She looks different. Older than before. The same as when I left.

A doctor in scrubs, without the mask is between her legs, talking to her, reassuring her, helping her. I am next to her, pain and smiles eminent from her, medication is helping her, and she watches the doctor. He is bringing a new life into hers. The soft noises are punctured by a new born baby's cry, and her smile lights up the room. It's a boy. He looks like pictures of me as a baby. She cries and asks if he is OK, settling her head back on the pillow, as a positive retort is offered to her question. I hear her say, Ronny, as I realise I am weeping.

Closing my eyes, the images disappear, the cry of the baby is toned down and gradually it's all quiet. I remain in this position for minutes, hours, eternity.

There is a new person in the group and they have reconvened, as I stand up and make my way over, I look forward to hearing their story and I genuinely want to help them. The coordinator is not here, I look around but cannot see her anywhere. The new person looks straight at me and asks

"Where am I? Should I sit down?"

China fills the void, as I do not seem to be able to offer quick enough response.

"You can take Marcus's chair, he found his route."

"Marcus? Who is Marcus? Bob was using that chair"

"Yeah sorry... Bob introduced himself as Marcus when he first got here, I forgot. He said he preferred to be called Bob, as that was what the Americans called him when he first moved there."